GREG'S HEART WAS POUNDING WITH FEAR

He waited a few seconds, then slipped out of his room. The living room was dark. But he could see Uncle Roy in the shadows. His uncle was reaching for something. His shotgun.

Bantam Books in the Triumph Series
Ask your bookseller for the books you have missed

THE BERMUDA TRIANGLE AND OTHER MYSTERIES OF NATURE by Edward F. Dolan
CUTTING A RECORD IN NASHVILLE by Lani van Ryzin
THE DISCO KID by Curtis Gathje
THE HITCHHIKERS by Paul Thompson
INCREDIBLE CRIMES by Linda Atkinson
ONE DARK NIGHT by Wallace White
PSYCHIC STORIES STRANGE BUT TRUE by Linda Atkinson
ROCK FEVER by Ellen Rabinowich

One Dark Night

BY WALLACE WHITE

PHOTOGRAPHS BY
BILL ARON

A Triumph Book

BANTAM BOOKS
Toronto / New York / London / Sydney

FOR DIANA

RL 2, IL 7+

ONE DARK NIGHT

A Bantam Book / published by arrangement with Franklin Watts

PRINTING HISTORY

Franklin Watts edition published Fall 1979
2 printings through July 1980

Bantam edition / October 1981

ISBN 0-553-14822-2

Published simultaneously in the United States and Canada

Bantam Books are published by Bantam Books, Inc. Its trademark, consisting of the words "Bantam Books" and the portrayal of a bantam, is Registered in U.S. Patent and Trademark Office and in other countries. Marca Registrada. Bantam Books, Inc., 666 Fifth Avenue, New York, New York 10103.

PRINTED IN THE UNITED STATES OF AMERICA

0 9 8 7 6 5 4 3 2 1

Chapter 1

Greg picked up the gun. He liked the feel of it. He glanced out the window at the street. It looked very hot outside, as if the buildings were going to melt.

"I told you not to mess with that gun," said his Uncle Roy.

Greg put the gun down on the desk. He swung around in his chair. Uncle Roy was the sheriff of Hill County. Everybody said he was as tough as a bull.

"It isn't loaded," said Greg.

"Don't mess with it anyway," said his uncle. "Not while you're in this office."

"I'm sorry," said Greg. He *was* sorry, too. He had always liked his uncle. Years ago, they had had fun together. And now Greg was going to spend the summer here. He wanted Uncle Roy to like him. He wanted them to get along.

Greg looked out the window again. Across the street, a boy was holding something shiny. The boy was very skinny. He wore shabby overalls. He was staring at the sheriff's office.

"Who's that kid over there?" Greg asked.

Uncle Roy moved toward the window. His face darkened. "Looks like one of the Lee kids. His family is trash."

Greg looked at the boy again. Trash? Greg wasn't sure what his uncle meant.

Now Greg saw that the shiny thing in the boy's hand was a wrench. The boy kept staring. Uncle Roy ran his fingers along his pistol belt.

"Why is he staring at us like that?" said Greg.

"Crazy, probably," said his uncle. He turned and started toward the back room.

Greg heard the door close. He was alone now. He felt puzzled. He didn't understand

Uncle Roy's attitude today, and he didn't understand the strange boy, either. He looked out the window again.

The boy's face was sunburned. He scowled, looking straight at the sheriff's office. Then, suddenly, he raised the wrench in the air.

He threw it.

It clanged across the street. It landed in front of the sheriff's office. The boy ran after it. He picked it up again, and Greg realized he was going to smash it through the window.

Greg jumped up and shouted, "Hey!" He ran to the door and opened it. "What are you trying to do?"

The boy's eyes met his. He glared at Greg. The boy seemed to hesitate. Then his eyes wavered. He turned and dashed off down the street.

Greg stood in the doorway. His heart was pounding. Maybe his uncle was right. Maybe the boy *was* crazy.

At noon, Greg and his uncle ate sandwiches in the back room. Greg didn't say anything about the wrench. But he asked his uncle about the Lees.

His uncle drank some beer. "Don't worry about people like that," he said. "They're no good."

Again Greg felt puzzled. Something was the matter. Something was wrong here, in this office. And out there on the street, too. He started to say, "But—"

"There ain't no *buts,*" said his uncle. "This is Danville. I know this town better than you do. If I say something, it's true."

Greg sat there silently. He looked at the glare in his uncle's eyes. His uncle was a big man. His face was weathered, and his eyes looked as if they had seen a million things. Greg knew he'd better not ask any more questions now. He didn't want any trouble with his uncle.

Trouble was what got him here in the first place. Greg lived in Memphis with his parents. He had a lot of friends, and he was good in school. But like a lot of other kids, he wanted to go out. To have fun. To explore things. At a party, some of the kids smoked marijuana. Greg was with them. They got caught, and then all hell broke loose. His parents were very upset.

Greg remembered how his father got on the phone, long distance. He called Roy, his older brother. His father had said, "Roy, I'm worried about my boy. I'd like to get him out of the city for the summer."

Uncle Roy had said that Greg could spend the summer with him, in Danville.

Greg hadn't seen Uncle Roy for nearly five years—since Greg was about ten. Aunt Sally was still alive then. She had been a wonderful woman. They had all laughed and joked a lot. And he and his uncle had gone hunting and fishing together.

But Aunt Sally died last year. And now Uncle Roy seemed changed somehow. He seemed harder, more suspicious. And there was a kind of coldness in his eyes. Greg didn't know what to make of it all.

He had been here three days now. He was staying at Uncle Roy's house. And he knew what he was expected to do. During the day, he worked in the sheriff's office. He was supposed to answer the phone and sweep up. At night, they would stay home and watch TV.

So far, things had been pretty good between them. It wasn't exactly like the old days, Greg thought. But maybe it was too early to tell. Just once, Uncle Roy asked Greg about the trouble back in Memphis. Greg explained that it wasn't his fault. Then Uncle Roy warned him—he'd better not get in trouble here in Danville. It was an old town, and a rough town. And Uncle Roy was responsible for keeping order.

Greg promised to behave.

Now Greg looked around. The sheriff's office was small. It was at one end of the main street. There were just two rooms—front and back. There was a jail cell, too. Nobody was in the cell. But there was writing on the walls.

One man had written, "Ain't no justice."

Greg and his uncle finished lunch, and then Greg went back to the front office. He had nothing much to do. Uncle Roy said he wanted to look at some property. He went out and got into the sheriff's car. Greg watched him drive off.

For a while, Greg read a sports magazine. Then he heard a car door slam. He looked up.

Orval walked in. Orval was the sheriff's

deputy. He had short hair and a potbelly. He used to be in the Marines.

"Hi, Champ," said Orval. "Want to help me out?"

"Sure."

"Go buy me some soda pop," said Orval. He handed Greg some money. "Make sure it's *cold*. Hear?"

Greg knew Orval loved cherry soda. He got up and headed for the door.

Chapter 2

Outside, it was like an oven. Greg could feel himself sweating under his T-shirt. He could see waves of heat rising from the street, like ripples. Beyond the town were the hills. They were bright green, all covered with trees.

Greg started down the street. He liked this little town. All he minded was being sent here as a sort of punishment. But the town seemed friendly enough. There was only one main street, and a few smaller roads leading out toward farmland. Greg saw some faces he recognized from before, but he also saw quite a lot of strangers. They were migrant workers, who came here from other places. They worked on the farms, and they stayed in a work camp up the road. When they got off work, some of the men would come into a cafe called Lola's, to drink beer.

Greg knew that his uncle and Orval didn't like the migrant workers much. They called them "outsiders" and said that they were a bad element in town. They said the migrants were all right as long as they stayed in their place. Greg had seen a few of the men walking along the side of the road. To him, they looked neither good nor bad. They just looked like a lot of poor people back in Memphis.

He walked past the clothing shop and then past Lola's. It was a small place with dark windows. He could hear a jukebox playing inside. He kept walking, past the courthouse and the filling station.

The grocery shop was at the end of the street. Greg went in and picked up a six-pack of cherry soda. The storekeeper was a gray-haired man named Mr. Coleman. Greg paid him, and Mr. Coleman gave him a Coke—free. Greg drank it, and they talked awhile. Then Greg went outside again.

At the filling station, something caught his eye.

It was the skinny boy, the one who had thrown the wrench. He had an old bike, and he was adjusting the handle bars.

Greg stopped. The boy looked up.

"What are you lookin' at?" said the boy. His face seemed even redder than before.

Greg walked over to him. "Hey, how come you did that this morning?"

The boy shrugged.

"How come you tried to bust the window?"

The boy scratched his cheek. "I reckon I don't know you."

"My name's Greg. My uncle's Roy Pierce. The sheriff. I'm spending the summer here."

The boy looked away. Greg figured he was about thirteen. Two years younger than Greg. The boy's eyes were pale. He had some teeth missing.

They faced each other.

Then the boy spat. Some spit landed on Greg's sneaker. The boy started to get on his bike.

Greg was startled. He grabbed the boy's shoulder. He spun the boy around. The bike fell.

"Let go!"

Greg was trying to stay calm. But he was confused. And he wanted to get to the bottom of this. He said, "Tell me what's happening around here."

"Let me go!" The boy punched him in the belly.

A wave of shock went through Greg. He dropped the bag he was carrying and heard the cans of soda thud. The boy put up his fists. He swung at Greg again.

Greg felt the punch in his stomach. It seemed to have come from nowhere. Greg didn't want to fight this boy. The boy was much too small.

"Tell me what—"

The boy hit him again.

Now Greg couldn't help himself. He hit back. The boy cracked Greg on the jaw. Greg reeled. He knew he shouldn't fight with a thirteen-year-old. But he was angry. Everything seemed to be happening at once. The boy swung

again. Greg slugged him. The boy gasped. He stepped back. Then Greg grabbed him by both arms. The boy's face was livid.

"Damn it, I only asked you a question!" said Greg.

The boy tried to pull away. But Greg held his arms. He had to find out what was going on. Finally, when the boy spoke again, he said, "I ain't talkin' to no Pierce."

"Why?"

"I just ain't."

"Tell me why."

Greg relaxed his hold. The boy looked so frail.

"What's your name?" said Greg.

The boy didn't answer.

"Look, I'm from out of town," said Greg. "I don't know anybody here. I don't want to fight you. I don't even *know* you."

A truck roared into the station. It was filled with hay. Suddenly the boy picked up his bike. He jumped onto it and pedaled off.

Greg reached down and picked up the six-pack. He watched the boy ride off. Why had the boy hit him like that? And why wouldn't he even talk to him? It just didn't make any sense.

He started back down the street. As he passed the courthouse, he heard a woman's voice.

"Hiya! You!"

He stopped.

"You there!" the woman said. She sat on the courthouse porch. He hadn't noticed her before. She was in the shade, fanning herself. Greg could see that she was old and very large. Rolls of fat shook on her neck. She was in a wheelchair.

"Come over here, boy," said the woman. "You shouldn't fight with Tommy Lee."

"I didn't mean to. I—"

"Listen to me," the woman said. "My name is Addie—Addie Blaine. I may be crippled, but I know a lot about this town. And I'll tell you something. I know who you are. And I know your uncle."

"Uncle Roy?"

"Roy Pierce," she said. "And if I was you, I'd get out of his house. Get out of this town. He's a bad one." Her eyes danced.

Greg drew in his breath. "I don't know what you're talking about."

"You know why Tommy Lee hates you? *Because your uncle tried to kill his pa!* That's why."

"That—That's not true!"

"Ain't it? Go on, now! Ask him!"

Suddenly the woman began to laugh. Her laughter rang out down the street.

Greg turned and walked away fast. The day was burning with heat. He was dizzy from the sun. And the woman's words seemed to burn, too. He couldn't believe it. Uncle Roy—trying to kill someone? Not Uncle Roy. Never. And the woman herself was strange. He had never seen anyone like her. A huge woman in a wheelchair. Fanning herself and laughing. And now Greg knew something was wrong here in Danville. And he had no idea what it was.

Chapter 3

All afternoon, Greg thought about what the woman had said. He couldn't believe it. It just wasn't possible. His uncle was a good man—Greg was sure of it. He wanted to ask him straight out: Had he tried to kill a man? But there was a hardness in Uncle Roy's eyes, a hardness that seemed to say, "Keep away."

His uncle was busy most of the afternoon. At about five, the two of them drove home. Uncle Roy lived about a mile from the sheriff's office, in a comfortable old brick house. It had a large lawn and was surrounded by cottonwood and red gum trees.

For dinner, they ate beef stew. Once, Greg

tried to talk about Tommy Lee. But his uncle changed the subject.

Finally Greg mentioned old Addie Blaine. He said, "She talked to me today."

Uncle Roy looked up sharply. "What did she say?"

"She said you—I—something about you and Mr. Lee."

"She said *what*?"

"About—about how you tried—to hurt him or something—"

"That old fool!" said Uncle Roy. "Do you know what she does? She goes out at night in that wheelchair of hers. She rolls around town, spying in everybody's windows. Then she makes up stories about people. Filthy stories. Lies!"

Greg wanted to keep on. He wanted to blurt out the whole thing. But everything seemed twisted now. Here was his uncle—his father's brother. And what the woman had said—he kept hearing her words in his mind.

But Greg didn't want to argue with his uncle. He knew it wouldn't get him anywhere.

He said, "I guess it's not important, Uncle Roy."

"You'd better not talk to her again," his uncle said firmly. And then he muttered, "She ought to be driven out of town."

After dinner, they sat down to watch TV. Above the sofa were two of Roy Pierce's hunting rifles and a shotgun. They hung on racks on the wall—mahogany racks that Uncle Roy had made himself. Uncle Roy was good at woodwork. He had a workshop out by the garage. Years ago, he had shown Greg how to use saws and lathes and other tools.

They watched a quiz show. Then they started to watch a movie.

The telephone rang.

"I'll get it," said Uncle Roy. He got up and went into his bedroom.

Greg could hear his uncle talking. Uncle Roy was saying, "Yeah . . . Yeah . . ." Then he said, "I'll be there." He hung up. When he came back, he was strapping on his pistol belt. Then he opened a drawer and pulled out his forty-five

"Where are you going?" said Greg.

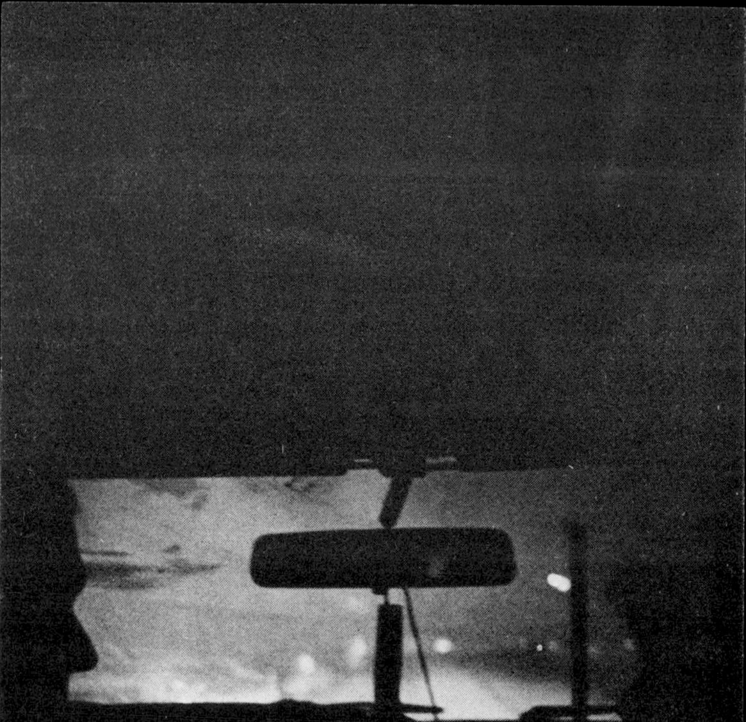

"There's trouble."

"Where?"

"Out by the old mill."

"Can I go?" Greg stood up.

Uncle Roy said, "It's a bad one. Some men broke into a house. They attacked a woman. Beat her up."

Greg knew this could be serious. But he said, "I've seen worse things than that." It was true. He had seen knife fights in the city. And once he saw a terrible car wreck.

His uncle looked grim.

"I won't get in the way," said Greg.

His uncle hesitated. Finally he said, "Well . . . if you keep your mouth shut. This isn't kid stuff."

Uncle Roy had a car and a pickup truck. The car belonged to the county. The pickup was his own. Tonight they got into the car. It was a black-and-white sedan with a red light on top.

They swung around several corners. Then they hit the highway. It was a two-laner, straight and dark.

Greg glanced at his uncle. Suddenly he remembered things that happened years ago. When he had visited Uncle Roy before. When they had had fun. There was a card game that his uncle called Red Dog. He and Uncle Roy and Aunt Sally would sometimes play it after dinner. They would get very excited over who was winning. Sometimes they would play until bedtime.

He remembered other things, too. One day he and Uncle Roy went fishing down by the river. His uncle seemed thoughtful, and he said, "You can learn a lot from the river."

Greg had asked him what he meant.

Uncle Roy had said, "The river is always changing. There's an old saying—You can't ever step into it at the same place. It's fresh and clear. But sometimes it gets muddy, and you can't see. There are rocks, rapids. You have to learn everything about it, Greg. Learn the currents and the hidden rocks. Learn where the fish like to hide. You've got to learn to be patient, too. Go look in the water sometime. You'll see everything there is to see."

Greg had said, "Aw, I just want to catch some trout."

They both had laughed.

He didn't know why he remembered that now. But he knew they had been closer in those days. They used to play catch together and go hiking together and roast hot dogs over an open fire. And once they slept in the hills all night in sleeping bags. In the morning, when they woke up, the sun was just rising over the mountains, and the sky looked like a thin sheet of glass. Greg wished that things could be like that again.

Now the car sped along. Soon they reached a small frame house. Lights were on inside. Greg's uncle turned into the drive. Orval's blue Plymouth was already there.

Greg and Uncle Roy got out. They went inside. A woman was sitting in an armchair. She was about thirty years old, and she looked pretty. But her dress was torn, and she was crying.

Orval was standing near a window.

"Are you hurt bad, Miss Jocelyn?" said Uncle Roy.

"I—I don't know."

"We'll get you to Doc James."

"Yes," she said. "They just . . ." Her voice sounded weak.

"What happened?"

Orval answered. "Couple of men broke in. Strangers. She says they talked like some of them migrants. They started to rob the place. She come home and surprised 'em. They figured they'd have some fun. They went and—"

"Hurt you bad?" said Roy Pierce.

"They—they—" The woman looked up. She touched her torn dress. Her stockings were torn, too. She glanced at Greg.

Greg felt awful. It looked as though she would never stop crying. He wished he could reach out and comfort her. She was hurt, and for a moment he felt as if he had been hurt himself.

He wondered what kind of people would do this. Miss Jocelyn looked like a nice woman.

And now she was sobbing.

Chapter 4

Orval stood there looking at Miss Jocelyn. He lit a cigarette. He exhaled a puff of smoke. Then he said, "They've got fifteen minutes' lead on us. I already phoned Luke Raskin and some of the others. They're on the lookout."

"Were they on foot?" Uncle Roy asked.

Orval nodded. "They didn't have a car. Probably walked over here from the migrants' camp."

"Then we ought to check out the camp."

"No, they headed east," said Orval. "They're probably going to get clean out of here, now that they went and did a thing like this."

"Well, they won't get far," said Uncle Roy. "Orval, you take Miss Jocelyn to the doc. You can catch up with us at Five Points."

Greg and his uncle went back to the car. They started down the road again. They drove slowly, and Greg kept looking out the window. He couldn't see much. But they passed a farm. There was a mailbox by the road.

It said, "Lee."

Greg stared at it. "Lee." He remembered that was the name of the skinny boy, and he wondered if this might be where he lived. He asked his uncle about it.

"That's them," said Uncle Roy. "They're a bunch of hog farmers. They never were much good."

But Greg took a good look at the farm. He would remember where they lived. Because he was starting to get more worried now. About everything that was happening here.

Soon Uncle Roy turned on the car's police radio. For a minute there was nothing. Then there was a report from the State Highway Patrol. But it was about an accident on Route 20, miles from here. And it had nothing to do with the men they were looking for.

They drove for another ten minutes or so. Haze drifted over the moon. The sky darkened. Then the haze passed, and Greg could see a crossing up ahead.

They came to it and stopped. Five roads met here—Five Points. For a while they waited and listened to reports over the police radio. Then a car came up behind them, and its driver honked.

It was Orval.

They started up again. They kept on in the same direction.

Before long, they came to an old black hulk. It was an old sawmill. Three other cars were already there, and several men were standing in the road. Greg's uncle pulled over.

They got out. The other men were about the same age as Greg's uncle. For a while the men stood there talking.

One of the men was small and wiry, with a sharp, high-pitched voice. His name was Luke Raskin, and Greg knew that he owned the clothing store. Raskin told Roy Pierce that he was pretty sure where the fugitives were. He said someone had seen them in a wheat field. He said, "They went into Anderson's barn. I think they're hiding there."

Greg wanted to say something. He wanted to ask—How did Luke Raskin know they were the same men? But his uncle told him to be quiet.

"All right," said Roy Pierce. "Half of us should take the river road. Half of us should head for Route 20. That way, we're sure to get them. Even if they try to swim the river."

The men got back into their cars. Luke Raskin and another man took the river road. Two more cars followed Greg and his uncle. This time they drove faster. They passed fields of soybeans and tobacco. Finally they came to another halt. A large barn loomed against the sky.

Roy Pierce switched off the engine. "You're staying in the car, Greg."

Greg thought he might be able to help. He

was agile, and he could move quietly. He said, "Listen, Uncle Roy—"

"I said you're staying in the car! This isn't for kids!"

"I'm not such a kid!" Greg said. "I'm almost sixteen!"

Suddenly his uncle slapped the steering wheel. "I shouldn't even have brought you along! You just get in the way!"

It was as if someone had hit him in the face. Greg felt angry and resentful. He didn't know why his uncle was acting like this. He didn't know what the others had in mind, either. But he knew something bad was happening. And he felt powerless.

His uncle stepped out of the car. Greg watched him and the other men through the windshield. He watched them start to creep up on the barn.

The men moved slowly. It seemed to take forever. Everything looked still. The men began to enter the barn. Then, suddenly, there was a cry. Flashlights went on.

Greg couldn't tell what was going on. Somebody shouted. He heard a cry, but no words. Then he heard another shout—a long shout, almost like a scream.

The flashlights played around wildly. Shadows flitted like ghosts across the landscape.

He heard some thuds, and then there was another cry. It sounded as if somebody was in great pain.

Greg put his hands on the dashboard. He leaned forward, trying to see.

Finally the men came out of the barn. They were dragging two men—two prisoners.

The flashlights played tricks on Greg's eyes. But he could see someone hit one of the prisoners on the back. With what looked like a club. The prisoner staggered.

Another man hit him with his fist.

Somebody yelled, "Bust you open for that!"

Then there was silence. The men dragged the two prisoners toward the road. They threw them into Orval's car.

Orval and another man got in. They drove off with the prisoners.

The others got into their cars and drove away fast.

Uncle Roy had a bottle in the glove compartment. He pulled it out and took a long swallow, gulping the liquor down. Then he floored the accelerator, and the car leaped forward with a roar.

The men in the barn—a scream—Miss Jocelyn—what Addie had said—Tommy Lee—Uncle Roy—everything was swimming around in Greg's mind. He wanted to wipe it all away.

He glanced at his uncle. His uncle's eyes looked glittery and cold. Greg gathered up his courage. He said, "Uncle Roy, you let them beat those men. *Why*?"

His uncle didn't answer. Instead, he picked up the bottle again and took another swallow. They were reaching a bridge. Uncle Roy pointed to a shack. His voice was shrill as he said, "*That's* where your old hag lives. Addie. The hag!"

Greg clenched his fists. He wanted to tell his uncle that he was confused and angry and frightened. But Greg was fighting back tears now. And words wouldn't come to his throat.

Chapter 5

Greg slept very badly that night. He tossed and turned. And he had strange dreams. The next morning he awoke very early, before his uncle did. He got up and dressed and made himself some toast. He glanced into his uncle's room, but his uncle was still asleep.

Then Greg walked all the way to the sheriff's office. It was a fresh, bright morning, and it wasn't too hot yet. But Greg couldn't get all those things off his mind. He kept wondering what he could do. Could he do anything at all?

When he got to the sheriff's office, he saw that the two prisoners were in the cell. They had been there all night. Immediately they began to talk to him. One was square-faced and well built. He said his name was Henry. The other was tall and thin. The only name he gave was Snake-Eyes.

Greg asked them if they were all right.

Henry said, "Listen, we didn't do nothing. We just got jobs on a farm up the road. You can ask the man that runs Camp Number Two. I'm from Chicago, and Snake-Eyes here is from Kentucky. We teamed up on the way down here. But we've only been here a couple of days. They didn't have any room in the camp, unless we wanted to sleep with the chickens."

"That's why we were in that b-barn," Snake-Eyes said. He spoke with a slight stutter. "We didn't have nowhere else to go. We just laid down on that hay, and the next thing we know, all them men busted in on us."

"That's right," Henry said. "I swear."

"What about over at Miss Jocelyn's?" Greg asked.

"We don't even *know* no Miss Jocelyn," Snake-Eyes said. "Miss Jocelyn—who's she? They got the wrong men."

Greg studied their faces. They looked scared, but they looked honest, too. Maybe they *were* the wrong men.

Greg was about to say something else. But Orval came in from the back room. He told Greg to stop talking to the men. Greg felt annoyed. It seemed as if Orval was beginning to boss him around all the time now. Then the phone rang, and Greg went over to the desk to answer it.

After about twenty minutes, Uncle Roy drove up. He came in and talked to Orval for a while, and Greg listened. The two men decided to take the prisoners to the courthouse, to be arraigned. Greg watched them open the cell door and lead the prisoners out. The men were handcuffed, and Orval hurried them along.

Greg sat at the desk and stared out the window. In his mind, he kept seeing the barn last night—the flashlights and the men being pushed around and hit with a club.

About an hour later, the men all came back. Orval led the prisoners back into the cell. He cursed at them, calling them names. Snake-Eyes cursed back. Orval shoved him to the floor—

hard. The man grunted. Then Orval slammed the cell door and locked it.

"You stay at the desk, Greg," said Uncle Roy. "Don't talk to those men, no matter what. Hear?"

Uncle Roy went into the back room. Orval said he was going over to Lola's—he liked to shoot a couple of games of pool before lunch. Greg sat and watched the prisoners. They were sitting on their beds. Sweat ran down their faces. They had taken off their shirts, and their backs were bruised. Finally he looked the other way.

After a minute, Snake-Eyes said, "Hey, kid—can we have some water?"

Greg swung around again. He didn't know if these men were guilty or not. He felt confused about them. And he felt bad about how they were being treated. Uncle Roy had said not to talk to them. But Greg had a mind of his own, didn't he? Finally he said, "OK."

He went over to the water cooler and filled two paper cups. He passed them through the bars.

Henry whispered, "Kid, you got to help us!"

Greg tensed his muscles.

"You *got* to!" Henry said. He grasped the bars. "You got to help us get *out*! Don't you know what they're going to do?"

Greg swallowed. He knew that the law would take its course. The men were supposed to get a fair trial. If Miss Jocelyn identified them, they would probably be convicted. Greg thought of Miss Jocelyn last night. Her torn dress. The way she cried.

But he thought of all the things he had heard, too, and what he had seen last night. Finally he said, "What can *I* do?"

Snake-Eyes whispered, "Everybody knows about your uncle around here. They talk about him out on the farms. We heard about him soon as we got here. They say he come near beatin' some prisoners to death last month. Him and his buddies. They've been takin' the law into their own hands. One man, they set fire to his clothes."

Henry tried to reach through the bars. Greg stepped back. Henry said, "You've just got to give us a break, kid. We didn't commit no crime. I swear. But your uncle thinks we did, and we don't stand a *chance* around here. They say they're going to make an example out of us, so the other migrants won't act up. There've been about three break-ins like this lately. Now they're trying to pin it all on us. If your uncle has his way, we won't be *alive* next week."

Greg's mind was reeling. He didn't want to listen to this. He didn't want to believe these men. He wanted to believe his Uncle Roy. He turned away and walked back to the desk. Behind him, he could hear the men whispering. They kept trying to get his attention again. He didn't answer them. He picked up a magazine and tried to read.

But he just couldn't concentrate anymore. It seemed as if something was building up all over town now—something dark and relentless, like a summer storm.

Chapter 6

At noon, Greg went into the back room. He told his uncle that he wanted to go out for lunch.

"Where are you going?" said Uncle Roy.

"I just want to walk around awhile." Greg didn't like to lie. But he had to find out a few things. He had to find someone who knew the truth, someone who would talk to him about it.

There was a man who might know the truth about one thing, anyway—Mr. Lee.

Greg went outside. He headed for the highway. He cut across a field. He passed a huge tree, a gnarled old oak. They called it the Dead Man's Tree. Nobody seemed to know why.

The sun was almost directly overhead. Greg looked up at the sky and blinked. The sky seemed to change more than anything else here in the country. Sometimes it was bright blue, at other times gray. And in the evening it was clear and pale. Now it was a metallic blue, with some clouds gathering toward the mountains.

Greg reached the highway and stuck out his thumb.

At last an old Chevy came along. It pulled over. A stocky, red-haired man was behind the wheel, and he said, "Climb in."

Fifteen minutes later, Greg was at the Lees' farm. It was old and ramshackle. The house was big, and it needed painting. A broken-down truck was parked near a shed.

A woman came out on the porch. She was thin, and her hair was long and lank. A little girl was with her.

"Mrs. Lee?" said Greg.

"Yes." The woman looked puzzled.

"I'm Greg Pierce. Roy Pierce's nephew. Can I talk to Mr. Lee?"

2318

"He's been sick."

"It's important."

The woman frowned.

The skinny boy came out on the porch—the one Greg had fought with, Tommy. He screwed up his face and said, "Get out of here!"

"I want to talk to your father."

"My daddy's sick. Get off this property!"

The woman put her hand on her son's arm, quieting him.

"Mrs. Lee," said Greg. "Do just one thing for me. Tell Mr. Lee I'm here."

The woman closed her eyes. Then she turned and walked back into the house.

Tommy Lee stood on the porch. His hands clenched the railing. After a minute, Mrs. Lee came back. She told Greg he could come inside.

Greg walked up the porch steps. A screen door led into the living room.

Mr. Lee was in an armchair. He was a lean man, with gray hair and penetrating eyes. His right leg was in a cast. There were crutches by the chair.

The woman went back onto the porch.

Greg sat down in a wooden chair. Now he would ask the question—the one that bothered him most. He told Mr. Lee what old Addie had said about his uncle. About how Uncle Roy had tried to kill Mr. Lee.

"Is it true?" he asked.

Mr. Lee smiled faintly. "Old Addie has a way of finding out things. She's peculiar, but she's not stupid. Anyway . . . a lot of folks around here don't like your uncle."

"I know that. But did he really? I mean—try to kill you?"

Mr. Lee frowned. "I wonder what would bring you all the way out here."

"Just what I say—I'm trying to find out what happened."

"Why?"

"Because—because I'm worried."

Mr. Lee shifted in his chair. He stretched his good leg out. There was a worn look on his face—he looked like a man who was stronger on the inside than on the outside. But there was something in his expression that appealed to

Greg. Suddenly he said, "Are you going to go tell your uncle you came out here?"

Greg hesitated. "I don't know."

"Him and me ain't exactly friends, you know."

Greg didn't know what to say. For a moment they just looked at each other. Then Greg said, "I only got here a few days ago. Then all these things started happening."

"What things?"

Greg wondered how much he should tell Mr. Lee. If he told him some of what had happened, maybe Mr. Lee would realize he was serious. He decided to tell him a little bit about last night—and about what the prisoners had said.

Mr. Lee sat and listened, tapping his fingers on the arm of the chair. Finally he said, "Things are just going from bad to worse, ain't they? Well, I'll tell you how I got this busted leg. But you won't like it. The fact is, I was walking down the road. Your uncle bore right down on me. He knocked me into the ditch. He was in that pickup of his. Going about sixty."

Greg said, "When?"

"Last week."

"But why?"

"Far as I can figure out, your uncle is scared."

"*Scared!*"

"He thinks I'm trying to get his job."

"You mean—sheriff?"

"That's right."

"But—"

"There's an election coming up here in November. A lot of people want to see him booted out. They say he's been getting too mean lately. Too ornery."

"But I don't—"

"I'm sorry, but it's true," Mr. Lee said. "Your uncle used to be a pretty good man. But now he's gone bad. It's a shame, too—a rotten shame." He shook his head. Greg could see he was in pain.

Greg told Mr. Lee how sorry he felt about his injuries. He said he hoped he'd be better. He asked if he could help. But Mr. Lee said no.

Greg left the house. Tommy and the little girl just stared at him, and Mrs. Lee didn't say anything. Greg started back to the highway. He wished none of this was happening to him. But he felt that he ought to do *something*. What, though? What *could* he do? Mr. Lee was injured. The prisoners were helpless. Old Addie was crippled. And Greg didn't know anyone else here who could help him.

Now, in the noonday heat, he felt almost sick. It was as if the whole town were beginning to boil. With hate and fear and the summer sun.

Chapter 7

That night, some men came over to Uncle Roy's house. They went out in the yard. They stood under a red gum tree, talking. Some of them were drinking beer, and some were drinking whiskey.

Greg's uncle told him to stay inside, so he sat in the living room. He tried to listen to the men outside, but he couldn't make out much of what they said. He knew that Orval was there. And so was Luke Raskin.

Now and then, the men's voices grew louder. They seemed to be arguing.

Finally the men drifted away. They got

into cars and drove off, and his uncle came back inside.

Greg asked him what they had talked about.

"Nothing much," said his uncle. "Just business."

But Greg didn't know if he could believe his uncle anymore. What kind of business could it be? He knew it must involve the prisoners. And he thought of everything people had been telling him. He felt as if *he* were the one caught in a trap, and he knew that from now on he would have to be very cautious.

Uncle Roy was acting as though nothing were wrong. He sat down in front of the TV set. He switched it on. "Tomorrow's Saturday," he said. "I want you to help me in the yard, Greg. You'd better get a good night's sleep."

Greg knew his uncle wasn't being straight with him now. He wished he could talk about the whole thing. He wanted to ask him what was really going on. But he was sure that if he did, his uncle would explode at him, and things might be worse than ever.

They went to bed early. Uncle Roy closed his bedroom door. Greg's room was right across from it. For a long time, Greg could see a ray of light underneath his uncle's door.

Greg left his own door ajar. He wanted to stay awake, if he could. But he was really very tired from the day. He lay in his bed. He turned on one side, then on the other. His mind was in a turmoil. Maybe this was all a huge mistake—maybe his uncle was telling the truth all along. Why should Greg believe Mr. Lee? Or Addie? Or the prisoners? Or *anybody*? It was as if everything was tangling and untangling in his mind . . . Tangling and untangling . . . Some stars were out . . . He saw them through his window . . . They were light-years away . . . Incredibly far . . . They seemed safe . . . They were so far from here . . .

He drifted off . . .

He dreamed. In his dream, he was on another planet. First there was no one else. Then he saw Mr. Lee. The man was bandaged. One leg was missing. His face was cut. Bloody. Horrible. He saw Greg. He chased him with a crutch raised high. The crutch was made of steel. Greg ran as fast as he could. The crutch sailed through the air like a knife. The planet shook. It exploded, and Greg was flying through space. He flew like a meteor toward the sun. He thought he would never stop. He was terrified.

He woke up.

It was dark and hazy outside, and now he couldn't see the stars anymore. He didn't know what time it was.

He heard something. A shuffling.

He blinked. Something was moving in the house. He pricked up his ears.

Then he slipped out of bed and went to his door. The sounds were coming from his uncle's room.

Greg blinked again. Now, in his fear, he was fully awake. He remembered what he had heard earlier, when the men were on the lawn. The words had frightened him. Something like "After midnight."

There were more shuffling sounds from his uncle's room.

Greg felt around for his jeans. He pulled

them on. Then he pulled on his T-shirt and his sneakers. He stood by his bedroom door and waited. After about three more minutes, his uncle's door opened. Uncle Roy came out of his room. He had on work trousers and a plaid shirt. He glanced toward Greg's room. But in the dark, he couldn't see Greg.

Greg's heart was pounding. He waited a few seconds, then slipped out of his room and took a few steps. The living room was dark. But he could see Uncle Roy in the shadows. His uncle was reaching for something.

The shotgun.

He watched his uncle take it down. He watched him go over to a table. Uncle Roy opened a drawer and took out something. It was a box of cartridges. Greg watched his uncle walk toward the front door.

Greg tried to think fast. He knew he couldn't go out the front. His uncle would see him. He went back into his room. He ran to the window. He pulled it open and slipped out quietly.

His uncle was already at the driveway,

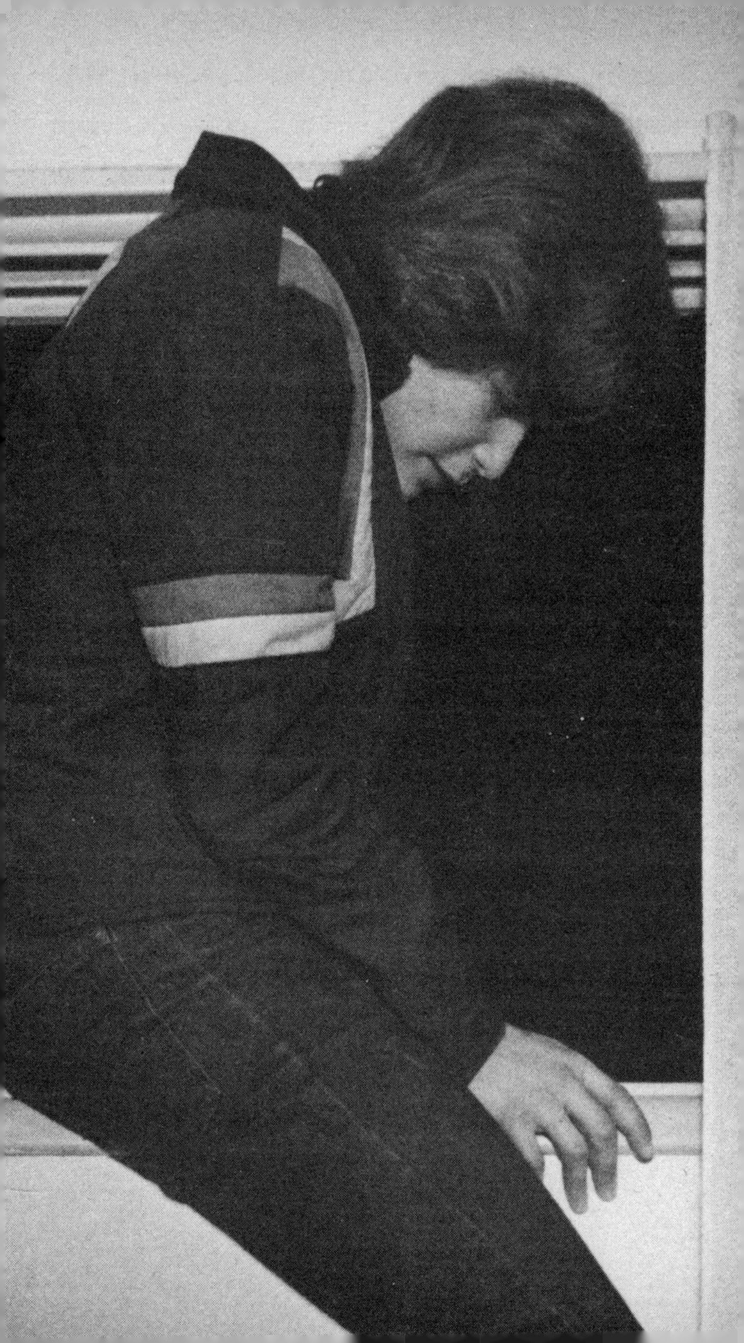

where the pickup truck was parked. Greg watched him get into it.

Greg crept across the lawn. He stayed in the shadows. He heard the engine start. His uncle hadn't turned on the headlights.

Greg was at the edge of the house. There was an open space between him and the pickup —bare concrete.

The pickup was starting to move. It was backing out of the driveway.

Greg knew he had to hurry.

His uncle turned his head away.

Now!

Greg made a dash for it. His sneakers made no sound on the concrete. He scrambled up into the bed of the pickup. He banged his knee and nearly yelled in pain. He bit his tongue. He had never been so frightened in his life. And whatever happened, he would have to be very, very careful.

He lay down on his belly.

Chapter 8

The pickup roared along. The road was bumpy, and the truck kept hitting ruts. Greg bounced against the metal truck bed. His uncle had turned on the headlights, and Greg could see their white beams in the night. He felt the truck make a couple of sharp turns, and he was thrown from one side to the other. He had no idea where they were going. He tried to sit up a little. He could see a quarter moon. It was low in the sky. The river was on the left. He saw rapids—frothy and white.

Soon they passed some houses. His uncle pulled over. He blinked his headlights. Greg stayed low in the truck bed. But he knew where they were now. They were at Luke Raskin's house.

Raskin was coming down the drive. He was carrying a rifle. He got into the front of the truck, and Uncle Roy pulled away from the curb.

Before long, they turned onto the highway. The truck picked up speed, and soon they were passing one of the camps where the migrant workers lived. Greg could see the outlines of shacks. He could see yellow lights in one or two windows, although he didn't see any people. They must all go to bed early, he thought. He knew that they were in the fields at dawn and that they worked until sunset. Once or twice, he had seen them trudging along the road at the end of the day.

In the truck's cab, Uncle Roy and Luke Raskin were talking. Greg tried to hear what they said, but he couldn't. He kept low.

Then the truck made another turn. For a while it sped down the road. Then it slowed down. And suddenly there was a rapid thud-thud-thud. They were crossing a bridge.

For another couple of minutes they rolled along. Then the truck slowed down again. His uncle made a sharp turn. Suddenly Greg realized they were passing old Addie's house. The one his uncle had pointed out the day before. Its windows were dark. Greg wondered if she was in there now, peering out at them. But even if she was, what difference would it make? What could an old woman like *her* do?

Now the truck turned onto a narrow road. They were going downhill. The road was very steep. And Greg recognized this road, too. He had seen it once before, years ago. The road led straight down to an old quarry.

The steep road took them down behind old Addie's house, into a gulch. Uncle Roy put on the brakes, and they went more slowly down the road. The brakes squealed as they came to the bottom. The truck stopped, and its headlights went out.

They were down in the quarry. It was cut into the side of a hill. For many years, men had dug rock here. But now it was worked out—abandoned. There were bits and pieces of rocks everywhere. In the pale moonlight, the rocks looked murky and dull.

Luke Raskin and Roy Pierce got out of the truck. Greg could hear their feet crunching on the gravel.

He glanced over the side of the truck. What he saw made him wince. There were three cars, and some other men were already there. They all had rifles or shotguns. And they had been drinking. He could hear it in their voices, and in their loud laughter.

"About time they got here . . ."

"Not going to get away with it . . ."

"You'll show 'em who's boss around here, Roy . . ."

A man offered a bottle to Roy Pierce. Greg saw his uncle put it in his mouth and take a swallow. Then he heard his uncle's voice clearly. His uncle held the bottle out and said, "Only the seven of us. Nobody else is ever going to know. I want your word on that."

"You can trust us, Roy," said another man. "It's the only way to handle it. We teach 'em a lesson, and the rest of 'em *might* just catch on."

"That's the truth," said Luke Raskin in his high voice. "Somebody's got to keep control. Somebody's got to be in charge."

"That's enough, Luke," said Roy Pierce. "Now where the hell is Orval?"

Greg shifted. His foot bumped the side of the truck. One of the men glanced his way. He winced. If they saw him . . .

The man looked away.

Ten minutes went by. Fifteen. The men finished one bottle and opened another.

Then another car came down the steep road. Its lights were off, but Greg could see it was Orval's blue Plymouth. Its chrome gleamed in the faint light. The car stopped. Orval got out, and so did another man. Greg was startled. Because the other man was Mr. Coleman—the man who had sold Greg cherry soda and been so friendly. His face looked grim.

Greg's uncle went up to the car. They opened one of the rear doors. Suddenly Greg

froze. They were dragging out the two prisoners —Henry and Snake-Eyes. The prisoners were handcuffed, and their faces were filled with fear.

Orval led them over the rough gravel. Their feet scraped and slid. Orval forced them along.

"What are you going to do?" Henry asked.

"Shut up," said Uncle Roy. His face looked mean—meaner than Greg had ever seen it. "You men don't think we're going to wait, do you? For some chicken-hearted jury to let you go? You broke into Miss Jocelyn's house. Attacked her."

Henry shook his head.

Snake-Eyes cried, "No!"

Uncle Roy kept talking. "One thing is clear around here—we take care of our own. Outsiders come in. People like you. Trash. Filth. You think you can act up. Do whatever you want with our women. But not here. You roughed up a real fine lady."

"Just let us go back to jail!" Snake-Eyes said. "We won't say nothing. Honest! We won't tell about tonight. Or b-beating us. Or anything. Just let us go!"

"Don't waste your breath," said Greg's uncle.

Henry said, "We didn't do anything. I tell you you've got the wrong men. You're making a big mistake. If you hurt us—well, you're going to regret it."

Uncle Roy took a long swallow from the bottle. He said, "I never heard so much hogwash in my life. We found you in that barn last night. Hiding."

"We weren't hiding. We were—"

"Shut up. It's pretty clear what kind of filth we're dealing with. Well, you know what we do with filth around here. We *scrub* it off, that's what we do. *We get rid of it.*"

"Please let us—"

"Save your breath," said Roy Pierce. He looked from one man to the other. "Do you boys know how to use a pistol?"

Snake-Eyes opened his mouth. But he couldn't speak.

"I asked you a question!"

Some of the other men began to murmur.

Greg's uncle waved his hand. He silenced the others. "Listen," he said. "We're all armed. You wouldn't stand a chance against us. But we're going to make it easier for you. We're going to let you go out like *men*—instead of yellow-bellied cowards."

Snake-Eyes began babbling. "We never done nothing. Honest. Let us go. We promise we won't say anything. Please! What are you going to do? Please listen! You *can't*!"

"Shut your mouth before I blast it off," said Roy Pierce. "You're going to put on a little show for us. Orval here is going to take off your handcuffs. You're going to walk over to the side of the hill. Then we're going to give you each a thirty-eight."

"No!"

Greg's uncle drank some more. He had begun to sway a little. "We'll have you covered with our guns," he said. "They used to hang people like you. But that wouldn't look too good, would it? So you two fellas are going to shoot it out. Right here. With each other."

Chapter 9

"No!" Henry's mouth was twisted.

Greg's uncle stood very still. He might have been a statue. Then he took another long drink. Now the bottle was empty. He threw it against a rock, where it crashed and shattered.

"But—"

Roy Pierce was getting louder. "Whichever one of you lives, we'll treat him real nice. We'll give him a little party. You like whiskey? We've got lots more. Then—Well, we'll put him out of his misery. Like the other one. We'll say you both got killed trying to escape."

Snake-Eyes made a wild sound. He tried to run.

Orval grabbed his arms. Luke Raskin grabbed him, too. They subdued him. He stood there panting. His eyes glittered.

Greg's uncle said, "You know something? You ought to be grateful. You won't even have to go through a court trial."

Snake-Eyes was mumbling. "Whatever we done . . . We never . . . Oh, Lord! I can't shoot at Henry! He's my friend!"

"Is he, now?" said Uncle Roy. "You should have thought of that before."

Greg took a deep breath.

Then he scrambled up and jumped out of the truck.

But before he had gone ten feet, someone grabbed him. Greg struggled. The man was big, and he had an arm around Greg's neck, choking him.

"What's going on?" It was his uncle's voice.

The other men whirled around.

The man was dragging Greg forward. Greg was kicking.

"Good God! What's he doing here?" said

Uncle Roy. "Greg! Dammit! How did you get out here?"

Greg kicked the big man who held him. He kicked him in the shins, and the man howled. Finally Greg wrestled himself partly free. He shouted, "You can't! I won't let you!"

"Don't you say one more word!" His uncle was standing in front of him. Greg could smell the alcohol.

"Uncle Roy! Stop it! You don't know what you're doing!"

His uncle slapped him on the cheek. Hard.

Greg fell backward.

"You don't know one damn thing about this!" his uncle shouted. "This is none of your damn business! You're nothing but a dumb kid!"

Greg felt the burn on his cheek from his uncle's hand. And now the man grabbed him from behind again. The man wrenched Greg's arm up behind him. Greg shouted, "Uncle Roy! Listen to me!"

Roy Pierce turned to Mr. Coleman. "Nick,

you take this boy over to your car. Keep him there." He pointed at Greg. "And I don't want to hear one more word out of you. You understand? Or I'll lick the daylights out of you!"

Greg's eyes stung. He felt as if there were a fire raging around him. He tried to struggle again. But Mr. Coleman and Luke Raskin had him by the arms. They dragged him over to Mr. Coleman's car. They opened the rear door and threw him in. Mr. Coleman stood beside the car door, with his shotgun.

Greg was breathing fast. He tried to scramble out the other door. But Luke Raskin had moved around there with his rifle.

Greg climbed over the seat, into the front. He opened the car window. He tried to see. His uncle was near the two prisoners, pointing his shotgun at them. He was forcing them toward the side of the hill. The other men stood back, pointing their guns at the prisoners.

The men made Henry stand on the left, by a large rock. They forced Snake-Eyes to the right, about twenty feet away. Then Orval walked up to them. He was carrying a rifle and a pistol. First he went over to Snake-Eyes and took off his handcuffs. He said something Greg couldn't hear. Carefully, he handed Snake-Eyes the pistol and backed away.

Then he did the same thing with Henry. He handed him a pistol, too, and backed away. He kept pointing his rifle at the men.

Greg's uncle stood back. He took a drink from Orval's bottle. He took a long swallow, and his voice was harsh when he shouted, "All right! I'll give the signal. Then we'll see how good you can shoot! On the count of three!"

Henry looked defiant. Snake-Eyes cried, "Oh, Lord! Lord help me!"

"All right!" Roy Pierce said. "Count of three! I want to see you aim real good. Because it's better to die quick."

Roy Pierce's friends were murmuring. Suddenly they all grew silent.

"One . . ." said Roy Pierce. "Two . . ."

Greg didn't care what happened to him anymore. Nothing mattered except what he had to do. He threw himself against the car door, and managed to push it open. He hurled himself out. Mr. Coleman shoved him back roughly. Everything was spinning around.

Suddenly a wild voice echoed. It sounded like "Yeeeaaaahhh!"

An apparition spun into view. Weaved its way down the steep road.

The men whirled. Their mouths gaped open.

A monster was coming. A monster in a wheelchair. Fat, wild, weird old Addie. She was in a red dress. Blood-red under the moon. Her arms were working. Her hands flashed as she spun the wheels of her chair. She weaved down the road, pumping with her arms. "Yeeaaaahhh!" she cried. "Yeeaaaahhh!"

"Grab her!" Roy Pierce yelled.

At the bottom of the road, her wheelchair bounced. She came to a halt. Just at the edge of the quarry. "I knew it!" she cried. "I saw you! I heard you coming down the back road!"

"Get that old witch!"

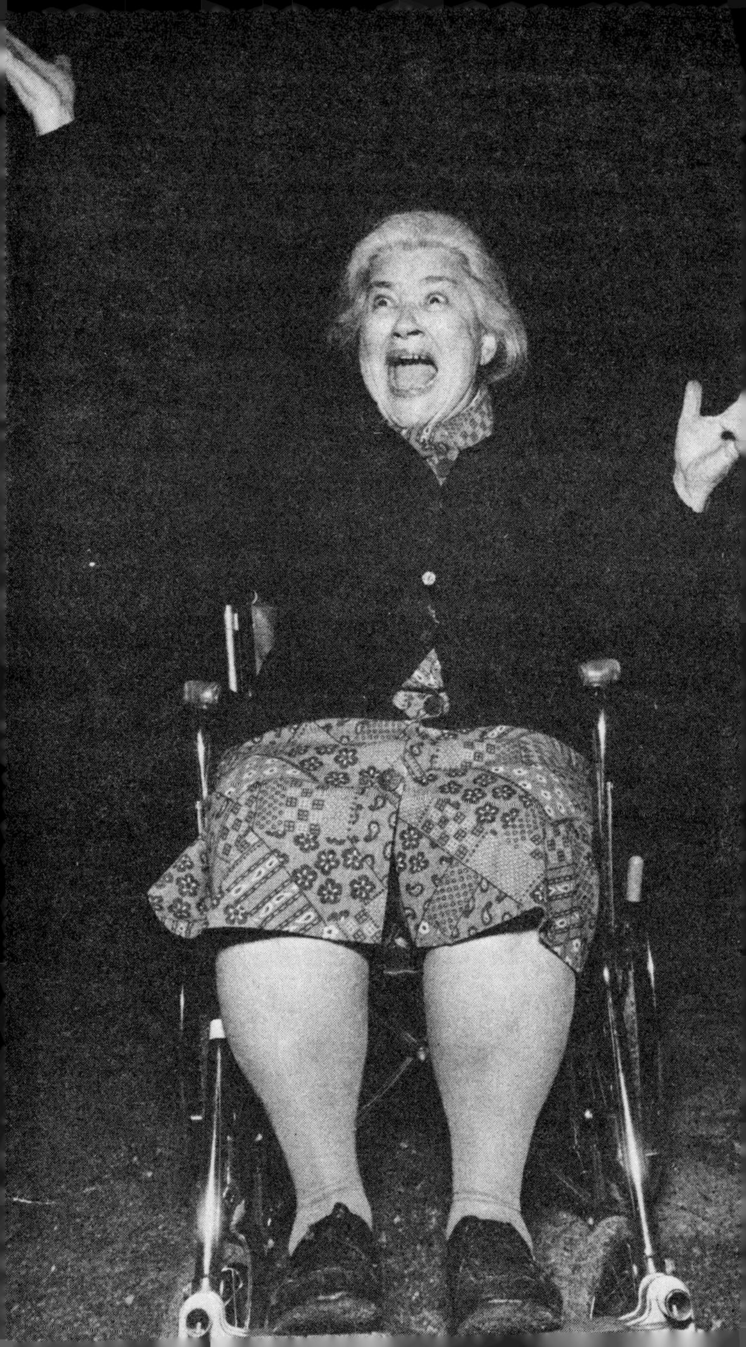

Two of the men grabbed her wheelchair. They handled it roughly. The crippled woman tumbled out. She hit the ground heavily, but she shouted, "You can't do nothing now! You can't! I got help! I'm not alone! Roy Pierce, you're through!"

"By God—" Uncle Roy turned. He pointed his shotgun. He aimed at Addie.

"Kill me!" she cried. "It won't make no difference!"

Roy Pierce stood there. For a moment, Greg was sure he was going to fire his shotgun. Greg shouted, "Uncle Roy—no!"

His uncle turned at the sound of his name. Then he aimed at Addie again. Then, finally, he lowered his shotgun. He frowned. "Pete and Chet," he said to two of the men. "Put the old woman back in her chair. Wheel her back up the road. When you get up to her house, give a yell. We'll have to decide what to do with her later. We've got a job to do down here."

"It's too late!" Addie shouted. "I told you I got help! I telephoned—they'll be here any minute!"

"Shut the old witch up," said Uncle Roy. He started walking back toward the prisoners.

The men picked Addie up. She was heavy, and she struggled with them. They started putting her back into her chair.

Roy Pierce took another drink. Then he said to the prisoners, "We're going to have our little shoot-out as soon as the old woman is out of here. All she did was give you a couple more minutes to live."

Henry said, "She's right—now you *can't* do this!"

"I can do anything I want," said Roy Pierce.

In the distance—headlights.

Cars came speeding down the steep road. Greg could see their white roofs and their flashing red lights. They screeched to a halt. Doors flew open.

Five men in uniform jumped out. They all had guns. One of the men wore a gold badge—a captain. They were from the State Highway Patrol.

The captain flicked on a spotlight. It flooded the quarry with brightness.

Uncle Roy and the others stood there, blinded by the light.

They had nowhere to run.

One of the officers ran over to Addie. She was sitting in her chair again, and now she smiled triumphantly.

"O.K., all of you," the captain said. "Put down your weapons. Or else get shot."

Chapter 10

There was a lot of talk about what had happened that night. Everybody in town knew about it. Everybody knew that Roy Pierce had been the leader and that he could go to prison.

Uncle Roy and his friends were arrested and charged. That night it rained. The storm that had been threatening for days finally erupted. There was thunder, and the streets were drenched. The next morning, the men were set free on bail. They could go home for a while to await trial.

Greg accompanied his uncle through the damp streets toward home. As soon as they got home, Roy Pierce telephoned Greg's parents.

Greg could see that it was hard for him to speak. Uncle Roy hesitated for a while before he told them what had happened. Then the story spilled out. He tried to apologize. And then his voice choked up.

Greg knew that his parents would be shocked. And he wasn't surprised when they said that Greg should come right back to Memphis.

But Greg talked to them for a long time. He told his father that he wanted to stay here till the trial. He told him that he was still very worried. And he told him that he might be able to help Uncle Roy. But inside, he knew why he really wanted to stay. Because he remembered things from years ago. He remembered when he and his uncle had been friends. When they had had good times together. He remembered sitting at the dinner table—he and Aunt Sally and Uncle Roy—and talking for hours on the front porch. How could he just walk off and leave his uncle now?

Greg's parents argued with him for nearly twenty minutes. Then, finally, they said he could stay.

"You don't have to," his uncle said.

"I want to," said Greg.

Uncle Roy looked terrible. He looked like a defeated man. Greg had a mixture of feelings —sorrow and anger and fear. Because he was still a little afraid of Uncle Roy. He wasn't completely sure whether his uncle might do something violent.

Roy Pierce had turned in his badge when he was arrested. Now the judge appointed another man to be temporary sheriff. There would be an election in a few months. Everybody said Mr. Lee would be elected the next sheriff.

Henry and Snake-Eyes were put back in jail. Even if they were innocent, there would have to be some sort of trial. Some people said that the men who really roughed up Miss Jocelyn got out of town two days ago. People said those men would never be found.

A grand jury met in the courthouse. They conferred for three days. Then the grand jury made an announcement. They had decided to charge Roy Pierce and the other men—

With disturbing the peace.

With reckless endangerment.

And with attempted murder.

Greg stayed at home with his uncle now. And for nearly two days, Uncle Roy hardly talked at all. They ate and slept and watched TV, and Uncle Roy seemed to be staring at something invisible, on the other side of the wall.

And Greg began to wonder whether he was right to stay. Maybe he should have gone back to Memphis, he thought. Maybe his parents had been right.

But then, gradually, Uncle Roy began to talk. He was sitting on the sofa one afternoon, in the living room. Greg was sitting across from him. Uncle Roy said, "Greg, I've got to talk to you about all this. I want to. But how can I explain it? It was wrong."

Greg put down the magazine he had been reading. He looked up at his uncle.

Uncle Roy held his hands out, as if he were trying to hold onto something. "I don't have any excuses, Greg. But let me try to tell you. I just . . . I'm sorry for everything. It seems like everything fell to pieces. A while ago. Last year. After your aunt died. She was sick a long time. I know it's not a good excuse. But it was more than I could take. It was like my whole world came to an end. I just didn't care anymore, about anything. I started drinking. Things got worse and worse. My drinking got out of control. And then everything seemed wrong with my life. I should have told your parents about it, Greg. I really should never have let you come."

In a way, Greg wanted to jump up and run right out of there. Everything was so painful.

But he knew it was important for him to stay—maybe for both of them.

And then he began to feel something new. Something strange. Something he had never felt before. Suddenly it was as if he were much older. As if he knew things he had never even suspected.

Greg said, "I think I can understand, Uncle Roy. I really think I can."

His uncle's face looked pale and drawn. He shook his head. Then he gripped his knees. "I'm not a very good man, Greg."

"But—"

"One thing I hope—I hope that you'll learn something from this. Please believe that. Even if you don't believe anything else I say. Because you're a good kid, Greg. I treated you very bad. Even if . . . Listen, you'll make your own mistakes. Everybody does. But maybe it's good you came here after all. Maybe you can learn from *my* mistakes."

For a while neither of them spoke. There was the sound of a train in the distance. Far off. A rumbling.

Finally Greg said, "What are you going to do, Uncle Roy?"

His uncle hesitated. "I used to be a pretty good carpenter. Maybe I'll go back to that. There's always a need for that kind of work. This town is going to be growing."

Greg stood up. "We'll get you out of this."

Uncle Roy shook his head. "No, Greg. Things don't work out that way. I wish . . . Well, we'll just have to live with it. With the way things are. The world is a pretty good place, really. It's men like me that make it bad."

"But you're still my uncle . . ."

"That doesn't mean I'm a good man."

Greg just stood there.

His uncle looked up at him. His uncle's eyes were glistening.

Greg went over and put his arm around his shoulder.

Chapter 11

Roy Pierce and the others were taken to court. The trial lasted nearly a week.

The county attorney was young and well trained and clever. He talked forcefully. He told the jury the men were dangerous. And he urged that they be sent to prison.

But the men had a good lawyer. He argued that the men had never been in trouble before. And he pointed out that Roy Pierce had already been disgraced enough.

The jury deliberated for three days.

The whole town waited. People stood in front of the courthouse, even though the storm had passed, and the sun beat down more strongly than ever.

It was as if the town were holding its breath.

Then, finally, the jury gave its verdict.

The men were all found guilty. Of disturbing the peace. And of reckless endangerment.

But they were cleared of attempted murder.

People said the men were lucky. They said it could have been much worse.

Before sentencing the men, the judge asked if they had anything to say.

Roy Pierce stood up in the courtroom. His face was pale, and his voice shook. He stumbled over some of his words. "I was your sheriff," he said. "I did the worst thing I could. I dishonored my badge. I deserve whatever punishment I get. Even though this has already cost me my job. And my self-respect. I just hope that, somehow, this will help somebody else."

None of the other men spoke. Instead, they stood looking down at the floor.

The judge pronounced the sentence. He put all the men on probation for a year. And he said they would all have to pay fines of five hundred dollars apiece.

Greg walked with his uncle out of the courthouse.

That evening, they called Greg's parents again. They told them what had happened. And this time, Greg told them he was ready to come home.

After dinner that night, Greg packed his suitcase.

While Greg was packing, Uncle Roy came into his room. He tried to smile. "You know something?" he said to Greg. "You're going to forget all about this. Just as soon as you get back to Memphis."

Greg knew this wasn't possible. "No," he said. "I won't forget it."

His uncle looked at him a long time. Then he shook his head and sighed. He rubbed his forehead and said, "I guess you're right, Greg. I really let you down, didn't I?"

Greg wanted to say something else—something hopeful, something that would sound right. But nothing sounded right to him. Not now. And all he could say was, "Yes. Yes, you did, Uncle Roy."

"Will you . . . will you come to visit me again? Someday?"

"I don't know . . . I'd like to."

"We'll sort of plan on it, then. Okay?"

"Sure," said Greg.

His uncle tried to smile again. He tried to make his voice sound cheerful. "Things will be different next time, Greg. Things will be a lot better."

"Sure they will," said Greg. But they both knew that this was only talk. Greg didn't know if things would ever be better for Uncle Roy.

They went to bed early and got up at 4:30 the next morning. Uncle Roy drove Greg to the bus stop, just across from the filling station. The sky was still dark. At 5:30, the bus came down the main street and stopped. There were only four other passengers on the bus, and Greg went to the rear. He found a seat and swung his suitcase onto the rack.

Uncle Roy was standing under a street light. After Greg sat down, he waved to his uncle through the window. His uncle waved back.

Then the bus pulled out. It rolled along the main street and made a turn. Looking out the window, Greg couldn't see very much. But he could make out the silhouette of the old Dead Man's Tree, alone in a field. Alone like an old ghost.

The bus swung onto the highway. It rolled along toward the bridge, where Addie lived.

Greg leaned back against the seat and closed his eyes. When he opened them again, he saw that the sky had grown lighter. He could see fields of wheat and tobacco. And in some of the fields, workers had already begun to arrive. Greg wondered if Henry and Snake-Eyes would be back in the fields again. And he wondered who all the other people were—where they came from, and where they were going.

But before he knew it, he would be home again. Back in Memphis, with his parents.

Things had turned out so strangely, he thought. The trouble he had been in before didn't seem like much now. And he realized that he was lucky he could go home—lucky to have a family who loved him.

He was glad to be leaving Danville. There was no question about that. He was glad to leave it all behind.

But he was sad, too.

And he wondered if he could tell other people things, like he felt different now. Older. And what he had learned. How everybody has troubles. And how everybody is a mixture of good and bad, love and hate, how nobody is all one thing or another.

Still, he couldn't really think very far ahead. Because he kept thinking about his Uncle Roy. How he was alone now, and lonely. And in his mind, Greg could still see him standing there waving.

And again he remembered things from years ago. When he and his uncle used to go down by the river. When they used to play Red Dog and go hiking together and laugh a lot.

The bus picked up speed. It rolled along beside the river. He looked out the window at the water in the early morning light. Rocks glimmered in the river. Rocks and pebbles and grasses. The grasses were swaying. Growing. Changing as the river changed.

The sun was just rising over the mountains. Across the river, a bird flitted out of the trees. It alighted on a log. It sat there for a few seconds. It pecked at the log. Then it was in the air again—soaring.

For a moment, the sky looked like a sheet of blue and amber glass.

And the river reflected the sky.

ABOUT THE AUTHOR

WALLACE WHITE was born in Utah in 1930 and spent most of his youth in California. He holds degrees from Stanford, Columbia, and the Sorbonne. He has written for numerous publications, including the *New Yorker*, the *Atlantic Monthly*, and *The New York Times*. Before assuming a career as a writer, he held numerous odd jobs—among them drugstore clerk, service station attendant, and taxi driver. He has traveled widely in Europe and the United States. He now lives and works in New York City. *One Dark Night* is his first book for young readers.

If you liked this book, here are some more great stories for you to read.

INCREDIBLE CRIMES by Linda Atkinson
Open this book and enter some of the most amazing crimes in history—including a man who received $200,000 in ransom parachuted out of a plane in a blinding snowstorm . . . and was never seen again. And a gang of small-time crooks who, after two years of planning, netted over a million dollars in fifteen minutes.

PSYCHIC STORIES STRANGE BUT TRUE by Linda Atkinson
Can people really read minds? See the future? Bend objects by just thinking about them? The stories in this book are certainly puzzling. Some are shocking. But can they be true? Read them and judge for yourself.

ONE DARK NIGHT by Wallace White
When 15-year-old Greg goes to visit his uncle, the sheriff of a small Southern town, he has no idea anything is wrong. But it soon becomes clear that trouble is brewing. And as Greg's worst suspicions are confirmed, a terrifying series of events thrusts him into a night of brutality in the darkness of an old quarry.

THE BERMUDA TRIANGLE AND OTHER MYSTERIES OF NATURE by Edward F. Dolan, Jr.
Mysterious disappearances in the Bermuda Triangle. The Abominable Snowman. UFOs. All incredible mysteries that have baffled authorities for decades. Are they science fiction or science fact? Read this book and decide.

Read all of these great books, available wherever Bantam Books are sold.